The Moon Pigeon

David Winship

For Bianca

Contents

Evil Lotion

Wilbur: Ladies and gentlemen, may I have your attention, please?

Pippa: Wilbur? Is that you? What are you doin'?

Wilbur: Please, Pippa. This is not easy for me. I need to concentrate. Ahem! Ladies and gentlemen of Trafalgar Square! Ahem, if I can just have your attention for a moment please, I'll get started.

Pippa: Seriously? We're pigeons, Wilbur! And I don't know if you've noticed, but these people aren't pigeon people. They're *'ooman* people!

Wilbur: Yes, well obviously I *know* they're humans, Pippa. I'll try to make allowances for them. I'm just finding it hard to get their attention at the moment.

Pippa: Well, you would, wouldn't you? They're 'oomans. And 'ooman isn't exackly yer first language, is it?

Wilbur: I'm sure they'll understand me if they just put their minds to it.

Pippa: Wilbur, you do realise they won't understand a word yer sayin?

Wilbur: They'll get the gist of it if I just use some facial expressions and a bit of body language to help express myself.

Pippa: Oh? What 'ave you got in mind exackly?

Wilbur: I don't know. Perhaps a few broad, sweeping gestures…like this.

Pippa: Hmm. That was actually pretty good, Wilbur. You looked jus' like the dyin' swan in that Swan Lake ballet fing. You know what? If you make a small 'op to yer left, you could do it fer real – the dyin' pigeon of Jellycoe Fountain. Tragic.

Wilbur: Leave me alone. I owe it to Phoebe to do this.

Pippa: Phoebe told you to do a dyin' swan in Jellycoe Fountain?

Wilbur: Of course not. But, as you know, I'm the official Recorder and Custodian of the Pigeon Chronicles of Trafalgar Square…

Pippa: You are? 'Ow did you get that gig?

Wilbur: Well, I… I just…

Pippa: Was you, y'know, elected?

Wilbur: Not exactly. I was... well, I was…

Pippa: Appointed by some kinda, y'know, panel of yer peers?

Wilbur: Um, no. I… I… Don't look at me like that! Somebody has to do it! Anyway, in my official capacity as Recorder and Custodian of the Pigeon Chronicles of Trafalgar Square, I think it's just right and proper that there should be a public proclamation of our appreciation for the pigeon who was responsible for restoring us iconic pigeons to this iconic London landmark. And I know Phoebe would have wanted humans to be involved in any such public... whatever I called it.

Pippa: Palpitation?

Wilbur: No, that wasn't it.

Pippa: Punctuation?

Wilbur: Public declaration.

Pippa: Well, that's *not* what you said. You didn't say nuffin' what sounded anyfin' like 'decoration'.

Wilbur: Yes, well, that's what I meant. And it's 'declaration', not 'decoration'.

Pippa: Wait, what are you doin' *now*?

Wilbur: Facial expressions. Obviously, I'm doing facial expressions.

Pippa: You look like one of 'em ventriloquist's dummies. Yer jus' openin' an' closin' yer beak.

Wilbur: Well, I'm a pigeon. When it comes to facial expressions, what *else* can I do?

Pippa: I don't know. But why are you tryin' to express these fings to 'oomans?

Wilbur: Because Phoebe was always keen to heal the rift between humans and us pigeons. She was a healing creature. She wanted to heal the conflict in our hearts and in our souls.

Pippa: What about rheumatism?

Wilbur: Rheumatism?

Pippa: Did she want to 'eal rheumatism? Some people suffer very badly wiv it, y'know. Whatever. Anyhoo, I don't fink any of these 'oomans is gonna listen to you.

Wilbur: See that thin human in the navy blue jacket? He just generously threw a piece of a hot dog bun towards me. I'd describe that as a gesture of encouragement, wouldn't *you*?

Pippa: 'E was frowin' it *at* you, Wilbur.

Wilbur: Nonsense. He's being friendly. Did you hear that? He just said 'hello'.

Pippa: Oh, my fevvas! He's on his *phone*, fer flutteration's sake! Listen, assumin' they *was* gonna listen to you, which they're not… what do you want to tell 'em about Phoebe, anyhoo?

Wilbur: I want to pay homage to her legacy and acknowledge the enormous importance of her exceptional achievements as an astronaut and spiritual leader. It should be a matter of public record.

Pippa: You wanna do *what*? You never called 'er a spiritual leader when she was *alive*. I can recall the time when you said she was a traitor!

Wilbur: No, I didn't. And even if I did, that was before I knew… that was before *any* of us appreciated what she was trying to do. Now please let me get on and tell these people her story. No more interrupting, please. Ladies and gentlemen…

Pippa: You're right. Phoebe should be segregated throughout Trafalgar Square.

Wilbur: Celebrated.

Pippa: There should be a legacy record in the 'ooman legacy records place where they play all the best legacy tunes. An' the song should be all 'bout what she's done fer peace. An' all what she's done in the world of space explanation.

Wilbur: Exploration, Pippa.

Pippa: But yer wastin' yer time wiv these 'ooman beins. They're not listenin'.

Wilbur: I think you're doing them a disservice. Humans are curious creatures…

Pippa: You're not kiddin'. 'Ave you ever

seen 'em doin' synchronised swimmin'?

Wilbur: No, I mean curious as in inquisitive. And they've got ears, haven't they? So, I think they *will* be listening to me.

Pippa: Yeah, but penguins 'ave got wings an' they can't fly.

Wilbur: Penguins? What have penguins got to do with it? Anyway, those are not wings. They're flippers. They originally had wings, but evolution determined that they needed to swim more than they needed to fly.

Pippa: What eggsackly is this evil lotion then?

Wilbur: Evolution, Pippa. It's a theory about how different species adapt to their environment by means of gradual, tiny inherited variations that enhance their ability to compete, survive, and reproduce. A famous human naturalist and biologist…

Pippa: Don't tell me! I know. Phoebe told me all about 'im. Darwin was 'is name.

James Darwin. An' 'e invented giant tortoises on the Galloping Islands.

Wilbur: I don't know what to say to that. Honestly, I just don't know *what* to say.

Pippa: Well, anyhoo, evil lotion doesn't work very well, does it? If I was a penguin an' a killer whale launched itself out of the sea towards me, I fink I'd want to fly, fank you very much! An' what if I was a penguin stuck on the top of Canada 'Ouse over there - yeah, I fink I'd wonder why evil lotion was, y'know, stoppin' me flyin'.

Wilbur: It's just the way it is, Pippa. Evolution makes the world go round.

Pippa: I fought *love* made the world go round.

Wilbur: Oh no. I sincerely hope not.

Pippa: Anyhoo, it doesn't make sense. Why didn't evil lotion turn penguins into fish? I jus' don't understand this stuff. Why don't *fish* 'ave flippers? An' while we're on the subject, why don't *'oomans* 'ave flippers? It would come in really useful, like when they're doin' synchronised swimmin'. No, never mind. You carry on. What were you sayin'?

Wilbur: I don't remember now. Ah yes, humans are inquisitive and they've got ears. So, they're going to be interested in what I'm saying.

Pippa: Okay, well why 'aven't *we* got ears? Oh, does that explain why *I'm* not interested in what you're sayin'?

Wilbur: Don't be silly! We *have* got ears. How else would you be able to hear me? We've got avian ears. They're behind your auricular feathers.

Pippa: Oh. I didn't even know I *'ad* curricular fevvas.

Wilbur: Auricular.

Pippa: That's what I said. Which ones are my curricular fevvas?

Wilbur: Those ones there - the ones in front

of your ears. Ha ha.

Pippa: That's really not funny, Wilbur.
Anyhoo, wevva I've got curricular fevvas
or not, I'm still not interested in what you're
sayin'.

Wilbur: You're not interested in hearing
Phoebe's story?

Pippa: No. Well, yeah. Yeah, I am. Phoebe
was my favouritest pigeon ever. Okay, *I'll*
listen to you, but I'm tellin' you – these
'oomans are not gonna listen. They're about
as interested as penguins at a flyin' display.

Wilbur: It's important to recognise our
heroes. Humans do it. Look at these statues
around us. What do you think they're here
for?

Pippa: I always fought it was to give us
pigeons somefin' to do. Y'know what I
mean? What we're well known fer?

Wilbur: Pippa! Really! No, humans
celebrate their heroes. You see that family
of humans over there looking up at the

statue of Charles I? Let me see if I can get their attention.

Pippa: Yeah? What will you do? Yer dyin' swan fing in the fountain? Hey, I know, let's try some synchronised swimmin'! That'll get noticed! 'Ere we go!

Wilbur: Don't even think about it! Stop it! Oh no! What have you done? I can't swim! Pigeons can't swim!

Pippa: Yeah, it's not as easy as it looks, is it? I fought *you* could *walk* on water, Wilbur! Try floatin' around fer a bit! You've got their attention now. Look, they're all flockin' round to see what's 'appenin'!

Wilbur: Hold out your wing! Help me get out of the water, please!

Pippa: Okay, okay, keep your fevvas on!

Wilbur: Oh flutteration! I'm all waterlogged! I won't be able to fly for ages!

Pippa: You'll be fine. At least you've got

yer ordinance now!

Wilbur: Audience, not ordinance.

Pippa: Listen, tell you what, I'll 'elp you. Between us, we can *act out* a lot of the story.

Wilbur: No, no, no. Oh, my feathers! What? Are you serious? We can? Oh dear, I've got a feeling I'm going to regret this. Okay, well, good evening to you all. Can everyone hear me all right at the back?

Apollo 10

Wilbur: Good evening, ladies and gentlemen, please join me as I take you back through the mists of time... Brrr! Aatchoo!

Pippa: That's it, Wilbur! The sneezin's a brilliant idea! Look, they're laughin'!

Wilbur: I hope you're satisfied, Pippa. I'll probably get pneumonia on account of you! Or bird flu! What if I get bird flu? Brrr! These humans might decide to have me put down.

Pippa: No, no, no, they wouldn't do that. They look like nice 'oomans. If you really get sick, I'm sure they'll give you some tweetment. Look, they're laughin'. Keep sneezin', Wilbur! Shiverin' too! Do some shiverin'! Like this. See 'em? They're jus' lovin' it! We've got 'em eatin' out of our 'ands now.

Wilbur: Wings, Pippa, wings. We don't have hands. And that's rather ironic – it's supposed to be the other way round. We're supposed to eat out of *their* hands. Aatchoo! But you're right – we've got a huge audience now.

Pippa: Get on wiv it then. Tell 'em about those mists of time again. We don't want 'em wanderin' off when there's mists of time around, do we?

Wilbur: Ladies and gentlemen, let us proceed through the tiny streets and winding alleyways of London and back, back through the mists of time, back to the Year of the Red Bus, in the Month of the Potato Moon, when Phoebe Featherbelle was born. I believe you humans refer to it as nineteen-ninety-something. What are you doing, Pippa?

Pippa: It's obvious. I'm pretendin' to be an egg.

Wilbur: How can you pretend to be an egg?

Pippa: I'm curlin' up all sort of small and keepin' as still as I can. In a minute, I'm gonna crack open some fevvas and be born!

Wilbur: Oh no. I knew I was going to regret this.

Pippa: Look! I'm bein' born! I mean Phoebe's bein' born!

Wilbur: Good evening, ladies and gentlemen…

Pippa: You've already said that about five times.

Wilbur: Have I? Well, ladies and gentlemen, allow me to extend a very warm welcome to you…

Pippa: Wilbur, can I do a bit of the introduction, please?

Wilbur: Well, I suppose so. Tell them we're going to recreate the story of Phoebe's life and...

Pippa: Good mornin', ladies and gentlymen. Join us, if you please, as we try to recreate one of the most misty 'istoric moments of recent misty 'istory. Our story begins in the very misty mists of time at the very beginnin' of Phoebe's life when no one could 'ave foretold what would 'appen to 'er, coz it was unclear. And why was it unclear? Coz of the mist I should fink. But as the mist clears, the true story of Phoebe Featherbelle will be reviled an' the actual inner secrets of 'er actual world will emerge in all their actual inner misty secretiveness usin', whenever possible, 'er actual words as they was, y'know, actually spoken...

Wilbur: Yes, thank you, Pippa, I think I'll take it from there. Phoebe Featherbelle, ladies and gentlemen, became one of our spiritual leaders, a resourceful and audacious bird, capable of pretty much

17

whatever she set her mind to. But the first few years of her life were humdrum and ordinary… Pippa, why are you circling around looking all pathetic, like a lamb in an abattoir?

Pippa: No, no, it's not a lamb. This is me doin' Phoebe bein' all ordinary an' 'umdrum. Coo-coo-roo-c'too. Coo-coo-roo-c'too.

Wilbur: *Now* what?

Pippa: That was my impression of what was possibly the very first words Phoebe ever spoke.

Wilbur: What? I don't think her very first words were "This roost is filthy. Look at it – feathers ev'rywhere!"

Pippa: Could 'ave been. She was a stickler fer cleanliness was Phoebe. Right from when she was jus' a little fledglin'. 'Er mum always used to make 'er tidy 'er roost before she was allowed out.

Wilbur: Ladies and gentlemen, as I was

saying, Phoebe was a pigeon who did whatever she set her mind to. In those defining early days, one thing she set her mind to was keeping abreast of what was happening in the world of you humans. Having learned both spoken and written English, she was always well aware of developments affecting us London pigeons. She it was who alerted the pigeon leadership to Westminster Council's byelaws banning the feeding of birds here in Trafalgar Square. In fact, she was instrumental in much of the protest activity that took place in the aftermath of the Council clampdown.

Pippa: Look! See what I'm doin'? There's some bread crumbs 'ere an' I'm shakin' my 'ead, refusin' to eat 'em! I'm protestin', see? I'm a beacon for pigeonism!

Wilbur: Okay. Moving on…

Pippa: Wait, hang on! If we're through with the protestin' stuff, is it okay if I jus' eat the bread crumbs? Can't 'ave a messy stage now, can we? Plus, Phoebe wouldn't 'ave liked it coz of the uncleanliness fing.

Anyhoo, are you gonna tell these people about what she done in the world of space explanation?

Wilbur: Exploration, Pippa. Now? You want me to explain about her moon exploration *now*?

Pippa: Yeah, it's excitin'. I want you to explore 'er moon explanation right now. If that's okay?

Wilbur: Yes, that's fine, but I'll have to tell them about Charlie Wallace.

Pippa: The NASA cyclist?

Wilbur: Scientist. He was a NASA scientist.

Pippa: I know. I remember 'im. I used to see 'im sometimes, tearin' down Charin' Cross Road, ridin' 'is bike.

Wilbur: I'll have to tell them about Apollo 10 and the moon pigeon too.

Pippa: That's fine. I'll do my moon rocket

impression. I've got Phoebe's moon boots back in the roost. Want me to fetch 'em?

Wilbur: I don't think so. Not now. Our audience will start drifting away if you go now. Ladies and gentlemen, a curious incident occurred during NASA's Apollo 10 mission back in the year you humans refer to as 1969.

Pippa: Yeah, why do 'oomans 'ave such a, y'know, borin' way of referrin' to years?

Wilbur: I suspect you humans don't necessarily celebrate Apollo 10. But we pigeons do! I'll try to tell the story from your human perspective.

Pippa: T minus sixty seconds an' countin'. We 'ave clearance to launch…

Wilbur: What are you doing?

Pippa: I'm gettin' ready fer my rocket impression.

Wilbur: I think you people referred to Apollo 10 as the dress rehearsal for Neil

Armstrong and Buzz Aldrin's historic walk on the Moon that took place a couple of months later.

Pippa: T minus 10 seconds. 9, 8, startin' ignition sequence…

Wilbur: The Apollo 10 mission objectives included a simulated descent to the lunar surface.

Pippa: Engines On. 5, 4...

Wilbur: Everything went perfectly smoothly up until the rendezvous between the lander and the command module.

Pippa: 2, 1, all engines runnin'. Oh-oo-oor! Launch commit. Hssss! Ch-ch-chop! Chop!

Wilbur: What *is* that noise you're making? Why are you clapping your wings like that? You sound like a pterodactyl.

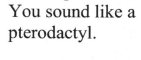

Pippa: Lift-off! Chop-chop-chop! We 'ave lift-off at

17:34 p.m. Eastern Daylight Time.

Wilbur: Oh, what's happened? Hmm. She's gone! Well, at least I can get on with the story without any more interruptions. So, ladies and gentlemen... suddenly, the movie camera operated by the astronaut, Eugene Cernan, picked up a pigeon moving above the moon's surface beyond the lander. And at that precise moment, the radar unit inexplicably failed. It was supposed to lock onto the command module prior to docking. But it didn't.

Pippa: Ready fer re-entry, 'Ouston. Standin' by to deploy main chutes.

Wilbur: Once the mysterious pigeon disappeared from view, the unit promptly began to function normally again, and a successful docking manoeuvre was completed.

Pippa: Oh wait. 'Ouston, we 'ave a problem. We don't 'ave any chutes! Look out!

Wilbur: Aaargh! Get off me! What are you

doing? Get off! Get off me, Pippa! Please!

Pippa: 'Ow weird was that?

Wilbur: You mean the radar unit failing when the moon pigeon went past?

Pippa: No, I mean me landin' right on top of yer 'ead!

Wilbur: Ladies and gentlemen, the engineers at the Mission Control Centre were baffled by it. In the absence of any available positive identification, they came to dub such sightings as 'moon pigeons', even though they didn't actually believe they *were* pigeons.

Pippa: Do you fink they liked my rocket impression?

Wilbur: Not now, Pippa. I'm trying to tell them there was an official NASA report about moon pigeons. So, yes, your NASA people drew up a report in which they attributed the Apollo 10 moon pigeon to either a piece of ice or a reflection from the window of the spacecraft. Obviously, they were totally deluded. It was a moon pigeon.

Pippa: Do you fink you could ask 'em if they liked my rocket impression? I could do anuvva one if they liked it.

Wilbur: Seriously, not now. Anyway, ladies and gentlemen, many of your fellow humans (NASA engineers and scientists included) were very dubious about the official explanation. One such sceptic was NASA engineer Charlie Wallace, who had always been intrigued by the controversy.

Pippa: T minus 10 seconds. 9, 8, startin' ignition sequence…

Wilbur: Please just ignore her. Wallace considered the report to be a prime example of official obfuscation and had always harboured an inkling that the moon pigeon had been a UFO piloted by aliens who had deliberately jammed the radar unit to deter you humans from attempting to land on the Moon.

Pippa: Chop-chop-chop! We 'ave lift-off at 17:54 p.m. Eastern Daylight Time.

Wilbur: Don't you dare land on me again!

Pippa: Oops! Splashdown! Don't fink there'll be any more flights this mornin'! Oh, fank you very much, ladies and gentlymen! Fank you. You're too kind.

Wilbur: I don't think they're applauding *you*, Pippa.

Pippa: Of course they are. That man over there is *whistlin'* too.

Wilbur: He's been whistling for the last hour or so. Now please let me finish this bit about NASA and the moon pigeon. Unfortunately for Wallace, his employers weren't impressed with his observations. Indeed, his views were considered to be incompatible with his contract, and he was dismissed from his position at NASA. Arriving in England a few months later, he disappeared after a night out with friends in the Charing Cross area. The various authorities lost track of him. After a couple of months, your Metropolitan Police people decided there were no realistic lines of inquiry left in the investigation. At that point, Charlie Wallace effectively ceased to exist… *Now* what? What are you doing behind that pushchair, Pippa?

Pippa: I've disappeared. Like Charlie Wallace. I've ceased to exist. Jus' ignore me.

Wilbur: I've been trying to do that all along… In fact, ladies and gentlemen, Wallace had assumed a new identity. Having obtained employment as a laboratory technician without having to present any formal qualifications, Wallace (now known as Glenn Mortaris) was living a secret life in an abandoned basement in South Kensington. In his spare time, he pursued his dream of sending an independent exploratory probe to the moon to investigate his theories about the presence of alien life on the Moon. And over the course of the next four years, he developed his anti-hydrogen rocket and launched it in 2007 with a symbolic occupant on board – our friend Phoebe Featherbelle.

Pippa: And so, on wiv the show! After this little song and dance routine, there'll be a short break for ice cream. I see some of you have brought some along. Yummy!

The Battle of Trafalgar Square

Wilbur: Naturally, that brings us to the Battle of Trafalgar Square. It doesn't really. Well, it *kind* of does.

Pippa: Yeah. In a vague, flimsy, not-eggspecially-connected sort of way.

Wilbur: You see, the two events happened simultaneously.

Pippa: Which two events?

Wilbur: Phoebe's moon flight and the Battle of Trafalgar Square.

Pippa: Oh yeah. You'd better explain.

Wilbur: Well, the two things were inextricably linked to each other in the sense that they both involved pigeons. Us London pigeons. And both events are linked to Phoebe.

Pippa: In a vague, flimsy, not-eggspecially-connected sort of way.

Wilbur: Well, yes, okay, I think I'll have to elaborate. I have to take you all the way back to the year you know as 2001.

Pippa: Through the mists.

Wilbur: What?

Pippa: You forgot the mists. The mists of time.

Wilbur: Ken Livingstone had just been elected Mayor of London. It was a dark day for us London pigeons. Dark, ominous and profoundly sad.

Pippa: And, y'know, misty.

Wilbur: Concern about potential health hazards and the damage to monuments caused by pigeon droppings prompted Livingstone to introduce a ban on feeding birds in the main part of Trafalgar Square... Pippa, why, for flutteration's sake, are you staggering around as if you're intoxicated?

Pippa: I can't see where I'm goin'. I'm lost

in the mists of time. Where are the monuments? Where is Ken Nibbleston? What are these dark, anonymous, sad shapes loomin' out of the mists of time? Is that 'im? Pleased to meet you, sir. Nibbleston, I presume?

Wilbur: Livingstone, Pippa. It's Livingstone. Anyway, his ban wasn't exactly popular even with you humans. Animal rights protesters and other sympathisers defied the edict and continued to feed pigeons on the square's north terrace. Fast forward to the auspicious Year of the Hawk. You humans know it as 2007.

Pippa: Coo-roo-grrr-grrrrr! Hey, do I look fierce? Guess what I'm doin'?

Wilbur: If that's meant to be a hawk, it's just terrible. Honestly.

Pippa: Wait. I 'aven't started circlin' yet.

Wilbur: So, eventually, in 2007, Westminster City Council extended the ban to the entire area. Violating the new byelaw became punishable by a draconian fine. Not satisfied with that, the Council enlisted the services of a Harris hawk and its handler to patrol the square from dawn till dusk.

Pippa: Look! I'm circlin'! Round an' round. Coo-roo-grrr-wheeee! Round an' round. Round an' round like I jus' don't care!

Wilbur: Despite the concerted efforts of a renegade pro-pigeon activist group of you humans known as the STTSP (Save The Trafalgar Square Pigeons) and, of course, our own resistance movement... Pippa, please stop, you're making me feel dizzy.

Pippa: But they're all applaudin'. Coo-roo-grrr-wheeee! Coo-roo-grrr-wheeee!

Wilbur: Bird numbers in this area were reduced by 75% in less than a year.

Pippa: Uh oh. I'm feelin' all queasy meself now. Uh oh.

Wilbur: Oh no. I'm so sorry you had to witness that, ladies and gentlemen. Really, Pippa, couldn't you have had a bit more consideration for your audience and done that behind the statue? No one's applauding *now*, are they? I think I'd better move swiftly on to the battle.

Pippa: Can you manage wivout me for a minute? I need to do a bit of urgent preenin' before I get into battle dress.

Wilbur: The Battle of Trafalgar Square was supposed to have been the battle to end all battles. Preparations went well until Phoebe fell out with the military wing of the pigeon resistance movement. Columbus, the Trafalgar Square Brigade chief of staff, being persuaded that Phoebe's knowledge of and acquaintance with humans would be a vital asset, convened a meeting with her. But Phoebe was deeply against the notion of us pigeons engaging in hostilities. And she told him so. She said she was simply not prepared to take part in the war effort as it conflicted with her deeply held personal beliefs. Violence begets violence, she told Columbus. He remonstrated with her, but in vain. Phoebe wouldn't heed his counsel. Mystified and exasperated, he issued her with an ultimatum: choose and serve her own kind or leave the Square for good. She elected to leave.

Pippa: Okay, I'm all preened and prepped fer battle! Look, my fevvas are all bristlin'! Coo-roo-grrr-grrrrr! Coo-roo-grrr-grrrrr! Take that, you swine!

Wilbur: Hey! Don't do that! Put your claws away! You're terrifying the human youngsters over there!

Pippa: I fink you'll find they're jus' enjoyin' the show.

Wilbur: That one over there is waving a plastic bag over his head to shoo you away.

Pippa: Seriously, Wilbur? No, he's showerin' us with food coz he's lovin' the performance.

Wilbur: I beg to differ. That's his mother's shopping.

Pippa: Nope, check it out - cheese, bananas, porridge oats, rice, breakfast cereals and a couple of pastries. Classic pigeon food an' no mistake. Yum!

Wilbur: You'd better take cover, Pippa – his mother's going to go for you with that umbrella! Sorry, ladies and gentlemen. So, where were we? Ah yes, Phoebe went back to work with Glenn Mortaris. Her absence in the Square was severely felt. Columbus accused her of consorting with the enemy. It's a pity Phoebe couldn't grasp the significance of the battle, but that's how it was. The rest of us knew we were about to draw a historical line defining the landmark moment when we pigeons finally rose up and challenged our subjugation and domination by you humans.

Pippa: It didn't eggsackly work out like that though, did it?

Wilbur: Well, that depends on your perspective. During the preliminary skirmishes, a crack squadron launched a poop attack on the hawk-handler. They also targeted a street cleaner in a yellow hi-vis jacket cleaning the base of one of the monuments. These pigeons were outstandingly courageous and specially trained to excel at flying.

Pippa: 'Ang on! 'Ang on! I fink I can 'ave a go at re-enactin' some of that contagious skirmishin'! Plus, *I* 'ave *also* bin specially trained to expel at flyin'!

Wilbur: Yes, I think we've seen quite enough of your expelling, thank you very much, Pippa. Anyway, ladies and gentlemen, despite these courageous exploits that are forever enshrined in the pigeon imagination, the raid was cut short when a sudden flash of lightning spooked the entire brigade.

Pippa: It wasn't our finest moment, was it?

Wilbur: It most certainly *was*!

Pippa: But the battle was over in just *five* minutes!

Wilbur: Yes, I know, but it was symbolic.

Pippa: That's what I'm sayin'. It was shambolic.

Wilbur: *Sym*bolic, not *sham*bolic!

Pippa: An' the 'oomans clearly won the battle - an' the war - wivout us doin' anyfin' to stop 'em. Eggsept fer a bit of, y'know, poopin', that is. It was jus' incontinent.

Wilbur: You mean incompetent?

Pippa: What does incompetent mean?

Wilbur: Inept.

Pippa: Okay, well, then, incontinent *and* incompetent.

Wilbur: It was a watershed moment. It shed new light on pigeonkind. No longer would we wilt under the heat of persecution or adversity.

Pippa: Whatevva. Anyhoo, you'd better tell 'em what the lightnin' flash was.

Wilbur: Well, yes, it turned out later that what had unnerved the birds had not been a meteorological phenomenon after all. It had been the vertical white streak of Glenn Mortaris's rocket, propelling Phoebe towards the Moon.

Pippa: 'Adn't you better tell 'em 'ow Phoebe and Mister Mortaris got togevva?

Wilbur: Didn't I do that already?

Pippa: No, you jus' said she was in the rocket.

Wilbur: Okay, well, Phoebe befriended Charlie Wallace, or Glenn Mortaris, as he became known, during the Year of the Famine. The pair collaborated for four years in the development of the condensed anti-hydrogen rocket that was supposed to propel her to a historic rendezvous with the moon pigeons.

Pippa: Wilbur, can I tell the ladies and gentlymen about anti-'ydrogen? Phoebe told me all 'bout it.

Wilbur: Well, I suppose I've mentioned it a couple of times now, so it might be a good idea.

Pippa: Yay! Thank you, Wilbur. Settle

down now, ladies and gentlymen. It's time fer some sinus-typical stuff.

Wilbur: Do you mean scientifical, by any chance?

Pippa: That's what I said. So, ev'ry type of particle has an ambivalent *anti*-particle.

Wilbur: You mean equivalent?

Pippa: I'm not sure. Anyhoo, it's got the same mass as the particle, but it's got the opposite electable charge. And when you put anti-particles togevva, you can make all sorts of anti-stuff.

Wilbur: Are you sure this is what Phoebe told you?

Pippa: Oh yeah. For example, you could put two anti-'ydrogen particles wiv one anti-oxygen particle and make anti-water. It would look like regular water, but if you tried to swim in it, you'd explode in a nice, invigoratin' splash of explodin' nuclear energy stuff.

Wilbur: I don't suppose you're going to act *that* out, are you?

Pippa: I don't fink so. And don't try drinkin' it, coz, believe me, it would be really anti-refreshin'!

Wilbur: I still don't think this is exactly what Phoebe told you. It doesn't sound very scientific to me.

Pippa: Sure it is. This is all very sinus-typical.

Wilbur: Scientifical.

Pippa: Eggsackly. Remember, I spent a summer at the LSE.

Wilbur: You spent a few weeks roosting on the roof.

Pippa: An' list'nin' to the sinus-typical conversations of the students when they fed me.

Wilbur: Do you even know what LSE stands for?

Pippa: Of course I do. London Stock Exchange.

Wilbur: No.

Pippa: Low Self Esteem?

Wilbur: London School of Economics. The students study *political* science there.

Pippa: Oh, please don't bring politics into this. You're jus' jealous coz I know sinus-typical stuff. Okay, now, where was I? Ah, yes. Anti-particles. So, if we put our minds to it, we could create an anti-you and an anti-me and we could meet on an anti-bench and you could throw me bits of anti-bread. And it might actually taste good!

Wilbur: At what point are you going to explain exactly what anti-hydrogen is?

Pippa: Yeah, I'm gettin' to that. Don't get yer fevvas in a twist! So, if you get one of them anti-electrons and put it wiv an anti-proton, the anti-electron orbits round an' round the anti-proton an' you get anti-

'ydrogen. An' you can fly to the Moon!

Wilbur: Ladies and gentlemen, I sincerely hope that helped.

Thirteen Chimes

Wilbur: I will now endeavour to explain what happened to us pigeons in the aftermath of the battle.

Pippa: Oh. Aren't you gonna explain what 'appened to Phoebe and 'er rocket?

Wilbur: I'll cover that a bit later.

Pippa: But we're strugglin' to keep these 'oomans interested now. Some of 'em are driftin' away.

Wilbur: Well, if they're not interested, they're not interested. Most of them are still listening intently. I'm feeling good about this now. Look, we've also got a growing audience of pigeons flocking around us here. They're enthralled by the story too. Even Phoebe's sister, Boomerang, is here with all her friends. This is good. Listen to them sing. Wonderful. Oh yes, they're like hearts with wings. Sad but beautiful and melodic.

Pippa: Coo-roo-grrr-grrrrr.

Wilbur: No, I said melodic. Anyway, I'm going to proceed by telling everyone about the thirteen chimes.

Pippa: Oh goody. If you're doin' the ferteen chimes, we'll 'ave to go all sinus-typical again! I'll do that bit. It's anuvva fing what Phoebe explained to me.

Wilbur: She did? Oh good grief. Well, you'd better get on with it then.

Pippa: So, it's all to do wiv consology,

cosnololy, cosma…

Wilbur: Cosmology.

Pippa: Yeah, what you said. So, fings are movin' through deep space away from us, yeah? An' that's coz space itself is eggspandin'. There are some fings out there whose distance from us is growin' so fast that light from them will *never* reach us.

Wilbur: And this has something to do with Trafalgar Square?

Pippa: Yeah, bear wiv me, Wilbur. So, the preservable universe, submergible universe, the opsapipple…

Wilbur: The observable universe?

Pippa: Right. The *obsavibble* universe will never catch up with the *actual* universe. Coz that eggspandin' fing is, y'know, eggshilaratin' faster all the time.

Wilbur: What has that got to do with *us*? Or the thirteen chimes, or anything?

Pippa: Don' fret yerself, Wilbur. It'll all become clear. So, at some point, we may be sittin' or perchin' togevva like this, an' then we'll notice that we've started driftin' apart! An' we'll 'ave to speak up. An' then after a while, we'll drift apart even more an' we'll 'ave to start shoutin' so we can 'ear one anuvva!

Wilbur: Are you serious?

Pippa: Oh yeah. An' on that day, everyfin' will get stretched out so much that even *sounds* will be affected. Big Ben will chime ferteen times at midnight. Yeah, so, that's it. That's what Phoebe discovered. That's the sinus-typical eggsplanation.

Wilbur: It's nonsense, that's what it is. The fable of the thirteen chimes has been part of pigeon folklore for generations. It's the scare story used by parents to keep unruly fledglings in check. As you know, many of us have a phobia about the number thirteen anyway.

Pippa: We do?

Wilbur: Yes, there's a name for the phobia. It's called triskadecaphobia.

Pippa: Oh, my fevvas! Are you serious? I fink *I've* got a phobia. What I've got is a phobia 'bout long words.

Wilbur: There's a name for that too.

Pippa: What is it? I bet it's a long word.

Wilbur: It's hippopotomonstrosesquipedaliophobia.

Pippa: My fevvas are itchin'.

Wilbur: Anyway, legend has it that the lion statues will come to life if Big Ben ever chimes thirteen times.

Pippa: Yeah, but Phoebe eggsplained the sinus behind it.

Wilbur: Well, that's just ridiculous, and I don't think sinus... Sinus? Oh no, you've got *me* at it now! Sorry, whether it's based on science or not, ladies and gentlemen, you simply need to know that the legend of the thirteen chimes is an old one like those stories about bogeybird creatures that hide under naughty fledglings' nests and grab at their tail feathers.

Pippa: Okay, so now *I* don' understand where *you're* goin' with the ferteen chimes fing.

Wilbur: I'll tell you. Remember I told you all about the STTSP?

Pippa: I remember. It stands fer Save The Trafalgar Square Pigeons. They're the lemonade 'oomans.

Wilbur: Renegade.

Pippa: I know. They're the ones that carried on feedin' us after the ban was imposed. They was always eatin' burgers an' drinkin', y'know, those sweet carbonated lemon drinks.

Wilbur: That's right. Well, during the months following the battle, the STTSP continued to defy the bird feeding ban. So, one day in the middle of the Month of the

Giant Sparkling Conifer, our military wing, the Trafalgar Square Brigade (we refer to them as the TSB), exploited the situation.

Pippa: Oh right, yeah! I get where yer goin' wiv this now - they spread that rumour, didn't they? They said Big Ben was goin' to chime ferteen times that night.

Wilbur: Yes, and it worked. We were all completely spooked, and we evacuated the Square for good.

Pippa: Coo-roo-grrr-rrrrroooooarrr!

Wilbur: What was *that*?

Pippa: That's my legendary lion impression. Coo-roo-grrr-rrrrroooooarrr! Be honest, Wilbur - you liked it, didn't you?

Wilbur: That was supposed to be a lion? It sounded more like a *sea* lion. A sea lion with a sore throat.

Pippa: Coo-roo-grrr-rrrrroooooarrr!

Wilbur: Really?

Pippa: Get on an' tell 'em 'bout 'ow the TSB did the eggsplodin'.

Wilbur: Exploiting. So, they cordoned off a no-fly zone around the Square.

Pippa: That way they could keep the food fer 'emselves.

Wilbur: Exactly. And within the London pigeon community, the TSB quickly became synonymous with intrigue, deception and cover-up.

Pippa: They was more than sinner-cinnamon-cinnamonous. They was evil. Tell 'em 'ow the TSB 'disappeared' people.

Wilbur: Yes, the few intrepid pigeons who tried to breach the security cordon were never seen again. Sorry, ladies and gentlemen. Please excuse me. This isn't easy for me – some of them were friends of mine.

Pippa: Take yer time, Wilbur. Come 'ere.

Let me put my wing around you.

Wilbur: Thank you. Thank you, Pippa. I'm okay now.

Pippa: Do you want to stop there?

Wilbur: No, really, I'm okay.

Pippa: Take a break?

Wilbur: No, no. I'm okay. So, anyway... Sorry. So, anyway, the TSB became increasingly alienated from the birds they formerly aspired to serve. Effectively, they created a Trafalgar Square republic separate from the rest of the London pigeon community.

Pippa: And that's when they became totally cinnamonous?

Wilbur: I just... I just never know how to answer a question like that.

The Lizard of Fes

Wilbur: Now we're going to backtrack slightly, ladies and gentlemen. I've got to tell you what happened when Phoebe left the planet in Glenn Mortaris's rocket.

Pippa: I don' fink I'll do anuvva take-off if it's all the same to you. I'm a bit worried 'bout my landings. I fink there must be a crosswind or turbulence or somefin'. I'll jus' do the sound effects. Oh-oo-oor! Hssss! Ch-ch-chop! Chop!

Wilbur: Pippa, rockets don't sound like helicopters.

Phoebe: Well, 'ow am I s'posed to know what a rocket sounds like?

Wilbur: There's a rumbling sound, followed by a kind of roaring slow-motion explosion.

Pippa: Go ahead. *You* do it, Wilbur! Do the sound of a rocket launch!

Wilbur: Well, I… Okay, well… Coo-coo-

woomph! Coo-coo-vrooooooooooooph-
fooooooooosh!

Pippa: Awesome. Ev'ryone *loved* that,
Wilbur! Jus' listen to that applause! Wow!
The boy wiv the freckles an' the green shirt
is practically jumpin' up and down. Do it
again, Wilbur!

Wilbur: I can't. I've got a sore throat now,
and my lungs hurt. It's not natural for a
pigeon to do this sort of thing. Even my
eyes have gone all funny. Let me get on
with the story, please, before my voice
gives out completely. As the rocket passed
over the far side of the moon, we believe it
was mysteriously intercepted, and Phoebe
found herself plunging back through the
Earth's atmosphere. She crash-landed in the
Mediterranean Sea.

Pippa: Is that *it*? Mysteriously antiseptic?

Wilbur: Intercepted. That's all I know.
That's all Phoebe told us, remember?

Pippa: Yeah, but are you gonna leave 'er
unfinkable encounter wiv the moon pigeons

as 'mysteriously antiseptic'? I assumed you'd done a bit of extra research or somefin'?

Wilbur: What research could I have done? Phoebe told us a lot about what happened after she crash-landed, but she didn't like talking about the moon trip. Personally, I don't think she even understood what occurred herself. So, I'm sorry, but I can only tell these people what she told us.

Pippa: Do you fink it was somefin' to do wiv moon pigeons an' aliens an' stuff?

Wilbur: Speculation is pointless. It's like seeing your great-aunt Hetty's face in a piece of toast.

Pippa: 'Ow do you know about my great-aunt 'Etty?

Wilbur: You mean you've actually *got* a great-aunt Hetty? I was just hypothesising.

Pippa: Well don't! It's not nice. And my great-aunt 'Etty wouldn't like it at all. Was you eyepoppersizin' 'bout the toast too?

Only I'm a bit, y'know, peckish.

Wilbur: Hypothesising. Yes, I was.
Anyway, let's get on. Phoebe's rocket ended
up in the Mediterranean Sea.

Pippa: Did she survive?

Wilbur: Well, *obviously* she survived! We
wouldn't have seen her and spoken to her
afterwards if she hadn't survived, would
we?

Pippa: Yeah, but these ladies and
gentlymen and people wouldn't know that,
would they? *They* don't know that we saw
'er afterwards. You 'ave to fink of yer
ordinance, Wilbur.

Wilbur: Audience.

Pippa: Eggsackly. Yer ordinance. You 'ave
to fink of 'em all the time.

Wilbur: She survived. Happy now? Her
feathers were drenched and her moon boots
weighed her down, but she managed to get
out of the rocket and she flew towards the

coast, eventually reaching the Moroccan city of Fes. She sought refuge in a crowded bazaar before exhaustion finally took its toll.

Pippa: Phoebe really liked it there, didn't she? She was surprised to find that 'oomans treat pigeons like royalty in Fes.

Wilbur: Hmm. That's true. The famous Chouara tanneries in Fes depend for their success on pigeons.

Pippa: It's about poop, isn't it? I know coz Phoebe told me.

Wilbur: Er, yes, it's about poop. The tanneries require an abundant supply of pigeon poop.

Pippa: Coz of the pneumonia, right?

Wilbur: Ammonia, Pippa. Not pneumonia. Ammonia helps to clean and soften the hides.

Pippa: So, you could say us pigeons – we're like a vital acid in the local ecology there?

Wilbur: Acid? Ecology? Oh, I think you mean an asset in the local economy. Yes, I suppose so. But life's not always a picnic for pigeons in Fes. It's probably worth bearing in mind that pigeon pie is a popular staple of Moroccan cuisine.

Pippa: Oh. So, yeah, actually it *is* a picnic for pigeons.

Wilbur: Anyway, Phoebe was discovered by an employee of one of the tanneries. And it's fair to say she was sympathetically nursed back to health and fitness. And she was treated like an honoured guest.

Pippa: Wilbur, let's 'elp these ladies and gentlymen imagine what Phoebe saw when she fell in love wiv life in Fes - which she did, coz she told me.

Wilbur: Well, of course, Phoebe always said she loved the snake charmers and was particularly struck by all the emerald green everywhere. There were mosques covered in emerald-green tiles, and palaces with marble arches and columns surrounding emerald-green pools.

Pippa: That's a lot of greenness. I like green. Paint the picture, Wilbur! I'll be a cobra! Coo-coo-hsssssssss!

Wilbur: Okay, picture yourself, if you will, wandering through the maze-like alleys, trying to avoid the donkeys and bicycles and mopeds and handcarts.

Pippa: Wait, are the donkeys an' bicycles an' mopeds an' 'andcarts all green?

Wilbur: If you like. Not the donkeys. So, eventually you come across one of the souks, where you find everything from incense to magic carpets and snake charmers. There are spice traders sitting cross-legged in front of small dunes of dried ginger, paprika, sea salt, turmeric and saffron.

Pippa: Coo-coo-hsssssssss!

Wilbur: No, no, Pippa. We haven't got to the snakes yet. And there are green handcarts piled high with green vegetables along with some dates and nuts and dried apricots and prunes. You hear an out-of-tune flute.

Pippa: Coo-coo-hssssssss!

Wilbur: Not yet, Pippa. You walk past stalls selling green bejewelled slippers, intricately designed green metal lanterns, green silk scarves and row upon row of jars containing brightly coloured natural dyes, mainly green. There's a tattooist sitting on a rug...

Pippa: Coo-coo-hsssssssss!

Wilbur: Not yet. A little further along, next to a pile of oily-looking rags is a woven green basket. The unmistakable raspy hissing of a hooded cobra can be heard... Ahem! The hissing of a hooded cobra can be heard... Ahem! Pippa!

Pippa: What? What is it?

Wilbur: I said the hissing of a hooded cobra can be heard!

Pippa: What about it?

Wilbur: Oh, forget it! Phoebe spent a few days enjoying her recuperation, inspecting the souks and the ancient palaces, mosques and monuments. One morning, she was slightly startled by the sound of a low-flying plane heading for the airport.

Pippa: There's an airport in Fes? 'Oomans are so bad at plannin'. Why did they build an ancient city wiv palaces an' stuff so close to an airport?

Wilbur: No, Pippa, the airport would have... Oh, never mind. Anyway, the sight of the plane encouraged her to spread her wings and explore the surrounding countryside. She told us it had everything - from jagged cliffs and misty snow-capped peaks to gently rolling terrains of all shades of green.

Pippa: Sounds really lovely. Specially the green trains. The ones at Charin' Cross are a yukky grey wiv, y'know, bits of blue and red.

Wilbur: She made good friends too. When she wasn't spending time with the family of the Chouara tannery worker who took her in and looked after her, she'd spend hours basking on the warm rocks in the company of one of the lizards. They exchanged stories of their respective worlds. Phoebe would show off her flying skills and he would demonstrate his ability to cling to vertical rocks. They would laugh and play together, Phoebe pecking playfully at his tail and the lizard hissing at her like water on a hot stove.

Pippa: Sounds wonderful. Was 'e green?

Wilbur: I don't know. Possibly. I don't think Phoebe ever said.

Pippa: What was 'is name?

Wilbur: She never mentioned his name. She just referred to him as the wonderful lizard of Fes.

Pippa: Why do you s'pose Phoebe ever wanted to leave the place?

Wilbur: I don't really know. I guess we all get homesick eventually. Sometimes you don't realise how much you love a place until you leave it.

Pippa: I love Trafalgar Square but I don't fink I'd feel 'omesick if I lived in a place like Fes. Sometimes I get, y'know, timesick.

Wilbur: Timesick? What's that?

Pippa: Well, I miss those times when I was younger - before I learnt to fly an' didn't 'ave to know such a lot 'bout the world.

Wilbur: Okay, well,… You do? Hmm. Anyway, before too long, Phoebe's thoughts returned to her friends back in London. With a heavy heart, she resisted the overtures of the friendly tannery workers who had so warmly befriended her and set out to tell the lizard she wanted to go home.

Phoebe: 'Ow did she know which way to go?

Wilbur: She didn't. The lizard suggested she should click the heels of her moon boots three times and just fly.

Fake News

Pippa: Wilbur, some of the 'oomans is driftin' away. We're startin' to lose our ordinance.

Wilbur: Perhaps they can sense what's coming.

Pippa: I doubt it. 'Ow could they? I fink it's coz it's startin' to get dark.

Wilbur: Exactly.

Pippa: What?

Wilbur: Oh, nothing. Anyway, Phoebe headed for home. After a long, arduous flight across eastern Spain, the Pyrenees and western France, she finally arrived back in Trafalgar Square, only to be captured by the TSB.

Pippa: Uh oh. Can we skip this bit?

Wilbur: Of course not. In a way, it's the most important part of Phoebe's story.

Pippa: Well, I don't like it. Do you mind if I don't do any actin' fer a bit?

Wilbur: Okay, but people have to know what happened. You understand, don't you?

Pippa: I understand. I'll jus' let you get on wiv it fer a while.

Wilbur: Are you okay?

Pippa: Yeah, it's jus'... It's nuffin'... I jus' don't like listenin' to what 'appened to Phoebe when she returned 'ome. It makes me sad.

Wilbur: Well, do you want to take a break for a while? I'll carry on without you.

Pippa: Is that okay? Are you sure? There are some fings what make me get all sensitive an' emotional an' mushy. You don' mind me mentionin' it, do you?

Wilbur: No, really. It's fine.

Pippa: Fanks, Wilbur. Fanks fer bein' understandin'. Y'know, yer the only one I can talk to about stuff like this. Yer the only one who really understands. You're such a good listener. Wilbur. Wilbur!

Wilbur: Mmm? Sorry.

Pippa: Seriously? Were you noddin' off?

Wilbur: No, no. I was just thinking about what you were saying. That's what I do when I'm listening and thinking deeply about something.

Pippa: Okay, well, I'll be goin'. Tell the ordinance an' ev'ryone not to worry. I'm gonna be okay.

Wilbur: Right. So, ladies and gentlemen, like I was saying - Phoebe got captured by the TSB... Pippa? I thought you were going?

Pippa: Changed my mind. That kid over there wiv the glasses an' the drippy nose 'as got one of 'em Big Macs, an' there's no way 'e's gonna finish it all!

Wilbur: Oh my feathers. Okay, so, Phoebe

told the TSB commander about the wonderful world of Morocco and how the humans, especially the tannery workers, really appreciate pigeons there.

Pippa: The TSB commando - that's Commando Awesome, isn't it? I remember you tellin' me 'bout 'im before. 'E flew upside down, didn't 'e?

Wilbur: Yes. By the way, it's Orson. Commander Orson. He also had a fear of heights.

Pippa: Not great fer a bird.

Wilbur: No. Not really.

Pippa: Did she tell 'im about the lizard of Fes?

Wilbur: She told him everything. She told him he should step out of his comfort zone and face towards new horizons.

Pippa: Like fly over to Souf Africa 'Ouse for a change?

Wilbur: No, don't be ridiculous, Pippa. She persuaded him that the land of the setting sun, as she called it, represented the holy grail for all the pigeons of Westminster.

Pippa: What's a 'oly grail?

Wilbur: A holy grail is something really special, something to aspire to, something that exists but is very difficult to find, something that involves a long journey. Phoebe told Orson that she would lead a mass migration of London pigeons to the fabulous city of Fes.

Pippa: 'E didn't like that, did 'e? Coz of 'is fear of flyin' an' so on.

Wilbur: That's right. He *certainly* didn't like it. But, of course, when the rest of the TSB heard about it, they thought it was a fantastic idea. Eventually, Orson took the view that Phoebe represented a challenge to his authority. He promptly ordered her incarceration. Severe injuries were inflicted on her scapula muscles, rendering her flightless, and she was held in confinement in a secluded roost overlooking the Square.

Pippa: Wilbur, yer usin' a lot of long words. I've got that 'ippo phobia fing again an' my fevvas are itchin'. An' it's not jus' me. The ordinance don't like long words. We're losin' 'em, Wilbur.

Wilbur: The bigger your vocabulary, the better you can express yourself.

Pippa: But, in your case, Wilbur, less is more.

Wilbur: What? Why?

Pippa: I dunno. Coz we don't like more. More is rubbish. Less is the new more.

Wilbur: Do you have any idea what you're talking about? How can less be more? More is more. Drat and flutteration! Now I'm talking as much gibberish as you are. Let me get on, please. So, ladies and gentlemen, as the days went by, rumours started to spread through word of beak that Phoebe was being held captive.

Pippa: The TSB denied it though, didn't they?

Wilbur: They did. Commander Orson was a cunning bird. He responded by tweeting fake news, suggesting that Phoebe was in cahoots with humans who were planning to round up all of us Westminster pigeons and dispatch us by ship and plane to Africa.

Pippa: Cahoots?

Wilbur: Cahoots is where you conspire secretly with someone.

Pippa: Oh, is that the name of the roost where she was bein' 'eld prisoner? But why was 'oomans in a secret pigeon roost?

Wilbur: No, cahoots isn't a place.

Pippa: You said it was. You said it was where Phoebe and the 'oomans was conspirin'.

Wilbur: No, they weren't conspiring at all. That's the rumour Commander Orson spread.

Pippa: If they wasn't conspirin', what was they doin' there in the Cahoots roost?

Wilbur: They weren't doing anything. Cahoots is not a roost. It's not a place. It doesn't exist.

Pippa: Someone jus' made it up? Is that why it's known as fake news?

Wilbur: Oh, my feathers! I give up.

Pippa: Don't give up now, Wilbur. We're closin' in on the eggcitin' bit. These people are gettin' restless, the shadows are gettin' longer an' I feel a bit of a chill in my fevvas.

Wilbur: Is that why you're pacing around in circles like that? Can you please stop doing it – it's very off-putting. You're starting to embarrass me and it's distracting people from the story we're trying to tell.

Pippa: But I'm cold. I've gotta keep movin'. You should do it too. It's okay - we can still tell the story at the same time. It's sort of aerobic story-tellin'.

Wilbur: Ladies and gentlemen, the rumours and fake news were leaked out for days, until two intrepid pigeons decided to do something about it.

Pippa: That was us, wasn't it? Me an' you? Did you say I was intrepid? Yeah, I like that. Intrepid. Oh yeah.

Wilbur: You don't know what that means, do you?

Pippa: Well, why don' you tell me, and then I'll carry on bein' it.

Wilbur: This is where a good vocabulary…

Pippa: Makes you a smarty pants?

Wilbur: No, this is where a good vocabulary comes in handy.

Pippa: Okay, let's not fight 'bout it. So, what does intrepid mean?

Wilbur: Fearless. It means being fearless.

Actually, no, it doesn't. It's not the absence of fear. It's the determination to fly forwards *despite* your fear.

Pippa: Oh. When you say flying forwards, does that include flying *away*? Coz I do that all the time – in a forwards kind of direction. Yeah, okay, intrepid. Go on, Wilbur, tell 'em 'ow we was so intrepid!

Wilbur: Well, it was early in the evening and we were flying north from Westminster Bridge. A thick fog muffled the sound of the traffic. Light from the ornate Victorian lampposts lent a hazy glow to the pavements. Do you remember? It was mystical.

Pippa: I remember the fog, but I don't remember Miss Tickle. Who was Miss Tickle?

Wilbur: Not Miss Tickle, for flutteration's sake! Let me use another word. It was mysterious.

Pippa: I don't remember *'er* either.

Wilbur: Who?

Pippa: Miss Teerius.

Wilbur: Oh, my feathers! Let's just get on.
So, under cover of the fog, we managed to
sneak into the Square without attracting the
attention of any of the hawks or TSB
sentries…

Pippa: If there 'ad been any.

Wilbur: Ssssh!

Pippa: What?

Wilbur: What are you doing, Pippa? Don't
give anything away just yet. I'm trying to
build some excitement and suspense here.

Pippa: Oh. Yaaawn. Sorry, it's gettin' late.

Wilbur: After scouting around for a while,
we came across the grim and foreboding
sight of Phoebe's prison roost.

Pippa: Cahoots?

Wilbur: Pardon?

Pippa: The grim an' forebodin' prison place – was it Cahoots? Was the roost Cahoots?

Wilbur: No, I told you Cahoots isn't... Listen, you were there. You were with me. Surely you remember that moment when we came across Phoebe early that evening in the fog?

Pippa: Yeah, of course I remember. Grim an' forebodin' it was. Grim an' forebodin'. Wilbur, can we skip this - I don't really wanna fink about it.

Wilbur: Well, I'll keep it as short as possible. I wouldn't want you to get all upset and distressed.

Pippa: Fank you, Wilbur, fank you. That's good of you. By the way, I meant what I said earlier 'bout you bein' a good listener an' all.

Wilbur: Oh, thank you, Pippa. I try to do my best. I appreciate you saying that. And I'm sorry I dozed off.

Pippa: What? You really *were* dozin' off?

The Tesco Bag

Wilbur: Ladies and gentlemen, we discovered Phoebe in a state of extreme weakness and emaciation. She was prostrate and delirious.

Pippa: Wilbur, Wilbur, please. My fevvas are itchin' like crazy. C'mon, no more long words.

Wilbur: What am I supposed to say, for flutteration's sake?

Pippa: Jus' say she was sick an' she couldn't fly.

Wilbur: Okay, she was enfeebled, debilitated and thoroughly incapacitated.

Pippa: No, no, Wilbur. Repeat after me: she was sick an' she couldn't fly.

Wilbur: Well, you've said it now and I just hope everyone is duly impressed, that's all.

Pippa: Wilbur, I do believe you're gettin' a bit shirty wiv me, aren't you?

Wilbur: Shirty? Shirty, my tail feathers! Certainly not. Not in the slightest.

Pippa: No?

Wilbur: No. Nnnngh.

Pippa: Wilbur, I nearly had to pry yer beak open to stop you snappin' yer wing fevvas. Calm down an' tell 'em about Phoebe bein' a prisoner in the Cahoots roost.

Wilbur: It's *not* the Cahoots roost! Nnnngh. Okay, okay, I'm going to stay composed and not let it get the better of me. So, we couldn't get any sense out of Phoebe. She just kept blathering ecstatically about the friendly tannery workers and the wonderful lizard of Fes.

Pippa: That's coz she didn't recognise us at first. She fought we was TSB pigeons.

Wilbur: Possibly. Anyway, there was nothing we could do for her without some help, so I left you - sorry, ladies and gentlemen, I mean: I left Pippa here with her. And I vowed to return with the means of rescuing her. Anyway, apparently, I'm not doing a very good job here, so... Pippa, perhaps you'd like to tell our audience what conversations the pair of you had while I was gone.

Pippa: No, no, you're doin' fantastic, Wilbur. It's jus', y'know, the long words.

Wilbur: Whatever. You can take over for a bit.

Pippa: Okay, fine. Wilbur?

Wilbur: Yes?

Pippa: Admit it, you kind of like me, don't you, Wilbur?

Wilbur: I do? To be perfectly honest with you...

Pippa: It's okay if you don't come right out and say it. I understand.

Wilbur: Oh, get on with it, Pippa. Tell them about your conversations with Phoebe.

Pippa: Conversations? Oh, yeah, okay. Well, obviously I wanted to 'ear what 'appened durin' the rocket trip.

Wilbur: Yes? And?

Pippa: She told me a lot of stuff 'bout space an', y'know, the Moon an' ev'ryfing.

Wilbur: Go on. What did she tell you?

Pippa: Well, I don't know if our ordinance 'ere will understand it. It's very sinus-typical stuff.

Wilbur: Humans understand astronomy and space. You shouldn't underestimate them. They have a long history of pioneering work in the field of science, going back all the way to when they invented the wheel.

Pippa: But they *'ad* to.

Wilbur: Had to what?

Pippa: They 'ad to invent the wheel coz they didn't 'ave wings, an' couldn't get around uvvawise.

Wilbur: Fair point. But they put a human man on the moon.

Pippa: Yeah, but we pigeons beat 'em to it. Even *they* know that. Remember Apollo 10.

Wilbur: I don't think these humans would concede that they lost to us in the space race.

Pippa: Why not? Even dogs and chimpanzees was flyin' in space before 'oomans was! Their knowledge of space is 'opeless. They admit they don't understand ninety five percent of it.

Wilbur: You mean dark matter and dark energy?

Pippa: Eggsackly. The 'oomans jus' imagine groups of stars as pictures in the sky. Consternations, they call 'em.

Wilbur: Constellations.

Pippa: We pigeons can *navigate* by the stars.

Wilbur: Not all of us. *I* can't do it and neither can you. Do you know if Phoebe could navigate by the stars?

Pippa: Phoebe? No, she told me not to spend too much time staring into space. She always relied on pages she'd ripped out of the AA Book of the Road. But *some* of us pigeons can use the stars. An' we can detect magnetic fields too. On the quiet, we're like little feathery flyin' quantum fizzyfists. An' we were on the Moon *first*!

Wilbur: Even if you believe that, you surely have to admit that humans have made great advances in space science and technology. Don't you?

Pippa: Nah. I fink we can safely ignore 'ooman discoveries about space. Until fairly recently, they fought the sun went round the Earth, as did the stars an' the planets. I'm embarrassed for 'em really.

Wilbur: Okay, that's true. I suppose it *is* a

bit embarrassing that for a long period in their history, they also believed the Earth was flat!

Pippa: It's not?

Wilbur: No, of course not!

Pippa: Drat an' flutteration! I've always dreamed of flyin' to the end of the world an' 'avin' a peer over the edge. I've been practisin' by lookin' over the edge of the National Gallery parapet.

Wilbur: Oh, my feathers. Okay, well, did Phoebe shed any light on her moon mission when you were talking to her?

Pippa: Yeah, of course. That's when she told me all about anti-'ydrogen an' the eggspandin' universe an' stuff.

Wilbur: I gathered that. And, of course, it's worth pointing out to the humans in our audience here that our pigeon brains can handle high-level thinking just as well as their human brains can.

Pippa: Better, surely? *Their* brains are stuck on the ground.

Wilbur: No, I mean we pigeons can muse about philosophy and comprehend abstract concepts like time and space.

Pippa: Well, we could if you used shorter words.

Wilbur: Yes, but the point is: humans don't realise we can do it.

Pippa: Why don't they?

Wilbur: Because when they contemplate abstract concepts, they use a part of their brains called the parietal cortex. It's part of their cerebral cortex.

Pippa: So, they can't fink wivout a skeletal corset?

Wilbur: Cortex. No. And we pigeons don't even *have* a parietal cortex.

Pippa: So, am I right in finkin' they don't fink we can fink?

Wilbur: Er, yes, I fink… I mean I *think* that's what I'm saying. But, anyway, let's get back to Phoebe. What about the Moon? Did she tell you *anything* about what happened?

Pippa: I'm not sure. I'm tryin' to fink. At first, I couldn't 'ear what she was sayin' to me. I remember I was jus' 'appy to see 'er beak movin'. When she found 'er voice, she told me broken wings simply mean you 'ave to find anuvva way to fly. Then she started tellin' me 'bout the cosmic order of fings an' 'ow all us pigeons an' 'oomans fit into it. She was very clever was Phoebe.

Wilbur: Yes, yes, I know, but did she give you any specific details about the Moon trip? I was gone for most of the evening. Are you absolutely sure she mentioned nothing about it?

Pippa: Let me fink. She said there are trillions of clusters whirlin' around the centres of superclusters. An' the clusters contain galaxies. An' stars orbit the centres of the galaxies, an' planets orbit the stars, an' moons orbit the planets, an' pigeons…

Wilbur: Yes? Go on.

Pippa: An' I fink she said pigeons orbit the moons.

Wilbur: What? Are you sure? Is that what she said? Think carefully. Did she tell you precisely what happened when her rocket reached the Moon?

Pippa: No.

Wilbur: Pippa, you know you just wasted everyone's time, don't you?

Pippa: Yeah, maybe. But I did it intrepidly, right?

Wilbur: Look around – lots of the humans have wandered away. Some of the pigeons have flown too. Boomerang's gone.

Pippa: She'll come back.

Wilbur: I don't understand why these people aren't more interested in Phoebe's story.

Pippa: It's disrespeckful, isn't it? They should be ashamed of 'emselves. We should go to the pigeon commissioner and complain.

Wilbur: What pigeon commissioner?

Pippa: You mean they don't 'ave a pigeon commissioner? You'd think they'd 'ave one, wouldn't you? Right 'ere in the Square, you can see they've got a 'igh commissioner of Souf Africa, a 'igh commissioner of Canada and a 'igh commissioner of Uganda. And in Trafalgar Square, of all places, they couldn't 'ave a 'igh commissioner of pigeons? That's terrible. If you don't 'ave a skeletal corset, you get treated like...

Wilbur: Like what?

Pippa: I dunno - like you've got a bird brain.

Wilbur: It's getting dark. I'd better get on with the story of Phoebe's rescue. So, anyway, while you were busy not learning anything about the moon trip...

Pippa: You're not gonna let up on that, are you?

Wilbur: Sorry. It's just that I *so* wanted to learn the answer to that question.

Pippa: I know. We all did. But most of the time I was wiv Phoebe, it was a question of liftin' the mood an' bein' encouragin'.

Wilbur: Yes, of course, she'd have been at a very low ebb.

Pippa: No, she 'ad to cheer *me* up. She promised me the future was gonna be better.

Wilbur: She did? How? Why? When?

Pippa: I can't remember all that. Wait, I fink I can remember the bit about *when*.

Wilbur: Okay, so... when?

Pippa: I fink it was... tomorrow. Yeah, she said tomorrow.

Wilbur: What? Okay, look, we should start describing her rescue while there's still some people left here. So, I left you and Phoebe, went back to the Ealing roost and rounded up a dozen or so of the strongest flyers I could find.

Pippa: And a Tesco shopping bag. Don't forget the Tesco shopping bag!

Wilbur: Yes, of course. The Tesco shopping bag was a crucial component of the rescue mission. By this time, the fog had cleared. But night had fallen, and we considered ourselves fortunate to have evaded the TSB sentries.

Pippa: If there 'ad been any. Oops! Sorry.

Wilbur: Please, Pippa!

Pippa: I said I was sorry.

Wilbur: We all endured a nerve-racking moment when we tried to roll Phoebe into the bag. Remember? We could easily have been spotted by a passing TSB patrol…

Pippa: If there 'ad been any… Oh, no. There I go again. Sorry.

Wilbur: I don't know why I bother. Anyway, nevertheless, we set off with a full moon illuminating our desperate attempts to carry Phoebe away from St Martin-in-the-Fields across the Square towards freedom.

Pippa: In a Tesco bag.

Wilbur: Yes.

Pippa: But disaster struck.

Wilbur: Yes. Phoebe's weight in the bag proved too much for us. She tumbled through the air and landed right here in the Jellicoe fountain, never to be seen again.

The Edge of the Universe

Wilbur: Well, ladies and gentlemen, I'm sad to say that we've arrived almost at the end of our ground-breaking, manifestly significant and intensely human account of the life and glorious deeds of the gracious and…

Pippa: Are you ever gonna get on wiv it? There's only two 'oomans left 'ere, an' one of 'em's fast asleep leanin' 'gainst a bollard. I fink 'e's 'ad one too many cans of discount lager. Oh, look! 'E's got a Tesco bag. I'll try to nab it so I can re-enact the rescue.

Wilbur: No, no, no! Pippa, leave it alone! Oh, my feathers! What are you doing? He's waking up, Pippa! Pippa!

Pippa: That wasn't nice, was it? It's a good thing for 'im there's no pigeon commissioner. I'd be reportin' *'im* for sure! Anyway, I s'pose there's no point re-enacting a rescue that didn't end up rescuin' anyone.

Wilbur: Yes, well, he's gone now. And that

just leaves the woman in the tartan shawl, carrying her umbrella.

Pippa: I fink she's jus' waitin' fer someone. She keeps lookin' at 'er watch.

Wilbur: We need to get her interested, Pippa. We need to up our game.

Pippa: Maybe you should do one of your big sweepin' wing gesture fings.

Wilbur: Ladies and gentlemen...

Pippa: There's no gentlemen left, Wilbur.

Wilbur: Ladies and...

Pippa: Not ladies. Just one lady. It's only *'er*, Wilbur.

Wilbur: Lady, please join us for the concluding session of our theatrical workshop celebrating the life and times of Phoebe Featherbelle.

Pippa: Are you now finally goin' to tell the ordinance lady that there was no TSB around when we dropped Phoebe into the fountain?

Wilbur: You just did. Actually, you gave it away a while ago.

Pippa: An' it was coz of Phoebe.

Wilbur: Yes, she'd managed to dupe, hoodwink, and outmaneuver them.

Pippa: I've no idea what that means. An' I suspect this lady don't understand you either. But first, perhaps you should say what 'appened to you after Phoebe fell in the water.

Wilbur: Do I have to? It's not necessarily pertinent to the story.

Pippa: Yeah, you really 'ave to.

Wilbur: Well, when we dropped the bag, there was obviously a lot of squawking and flapping and I became disorientated.

Pippa: Panic-stricken.

Wilbur: Disorientated.

Pippa: And you flew through the door of Café Nero.

Wilbur: Er, yes.

Pippa: Well, go on.

Wilbur: No, that's it.

Pippa: No, it's not. You collided wiv a cup of latte and a tomato and mozzarella panini. 'Ow was the coffee, by the way?

Wilbur: Scaldingly hot. I got quite badly burned. Which is why I didn't make it to the fountain before poor Phoebe's waterlogged body was scooped out by the humans.

Pippa: Yer forgettin' somefin'. I came to your aid, remember?

Wilbur: Yes, that was remiss of me. Sorry. Thank you for being there for me.

Pippa: You're welcome. I was quite

concerned about you, until I saw you tuckin' into that panini.

Wilbur: No, that's not how it was at all.

Pippa: You 'ad panini crumbs all over yer beak.

Wilbur: That's not fair. I... I had to apply something cool to the blisters.

Pippa: Hmm.

Wilbur: Anyway, I've been meaning to ask you something. Why did you fly into Café Nero after me, when you could have flown to the fountain to help Phoebe?

Pippa: I dunno. I didn't 'ave time to fink. You both needed my 'elp an' I didn't know what to do. I jus' found meself next to you in the café.

Wilbur: I don't know what to say.

Pippa: Neeva do I. You'd better get on wiv the story.

Wilbur: Well, as far as we could ascertain, Phoebe drowned and was fished out of the water by one of the humans. Please don't cry like that, Pippa. Here, let me comfort you.

Pippa: [sniff] Fank you, Wilbur. Put yer wing round me. [sniff] A bit tighter. Fank you. That's not the end of Phoebe's story though, is it? [sniff]

Wilbur: No, it's not. After spending an uncomfortable night roosting under a bench, we all woke up to find that the Harris hawk and its handler were conspicuous by their absence.

Pippa: And there were no TSB patrols.

Wilbur: Look, the woman with the shawl is taking a picture of us with her phone.

Pippa: Oh no. Oh, my fevvas. I'm all sniffly an' I 'aven't done any preenin' for hours.

Wilbur: So, anyway, we ran into the sister of one of the TSB guards and she told us what had happened. Remember earlier when I was saying about Phoebe conspiring with humans to send pigeons off to Morocco?

Pippa: Yeah, that's right - Commando Awesome's fake news.

Wilbur: In fact, Orson had been taken in by Phoebe's tales of the charmed life enjoyed by the pigeons in Fes...

Pippa: An' 'e was plannin' to go there 'imself!

Wilbur: Right. He'd been plotting a complete exodus of the TSB to pigeon nirvana.

Pippa: *What* accidents?

Wilbur: Exodus. It's like a mass departure.

Pippa: The TSB were gonna leave to go to a pigeon rock concert?

Wilbur: No! Oh my feathers! Nirvana is a place of perfect peace and happiness, like heaven. Forget it - they were going to Fes.

Pippa: Oh, I've jus' remembered somefin'. Somefin' important. I've remembered what Phoebe told me when I spiffic...spellific...spessfickily...

Wilbur: Specifically?

Pippa: Yeah, fanks... when I spessfickily asked 'er 'bout the moon trip.

Wilbur: Well, go on. What did she say?

Pippa: It's not much really. An' I didn't understand it. Now I fink 'bout it, it's no wonder I forgot 'bout it.

Wilbur: Come on, Pippa, what did she say?

Pippa: She said: "Though you fly t'wards the edge of the universe, the universe will just fly wiv you. And when you arrive, you won't 'ave left. My 'ighest aspirations simply take me 'ome."

Wilbur: Oh, my feathers.

Pippa: Uh? What?

Wilbur: Wait, wait. I need to think about that.

Pippa: You do? Well, I suggest you 'urry up, coz that woman 'as put 'er phone away and I fink she's goin'.

Wilbur: Okay. The entire brigade had departed for Fes a couple of days before we attempted our rescue.

Pippa: So, there were no pigeons left in Trafalgar Square. None at all.

Wilbur: Which left the hawk and its handler redundant…

Pippa: …An' the 'oomans were un'appy 'bout there bein' no pigeons. An' they complained to the council people…

Wilbur: … And the feeding ban was lifted. Trafalgar Square was slowly reclaimed by us pigeons returning from exile. The humans, who had become nostalgic for the age-old practice of feeding us in the

Square, welcomed us back. And we all started to enjoy life here once again!

Pippa: Yay! Oh, the lady's goin'. Goodbye, lady. 'Ope you liked the story! Tell all yer friends!

Wilbur: Well, Pippa, I guess we're done. The lady's gone. The pigeons have all flown to roost. Boomerang never came back.

Pippa: It's jus' us two. Wilbur?

Wilbur: Yes?

Pippa: So, all the stuff that 'appened… it was all Phoebe's idea, wasn't it?

Wilbur: Yes, she engineered the whole thing. She fooled Orson and the TSB into leaving the Square…

Pippa: … An' she made *everyone* 'appy. Even the TSB!

Wilbur: I guess so. There's every reason to assume they're enjoying life right now in the wonderful land of Fes.

Pippa: Assumin' they're avoidin' the picnics anyhoo! Do you fink even Commando Awesome is 'appy?

Wilbur: Well, I don't know if someone like Orson could *ever* be happy.

Pippa: Maybe if 'e flew right on past Morocco and went all the way to Australia?

Wilbur: Why Australia?

Pippa: Coz then 'e would be flyin' the right way up! Ha ha. Coo-coo-roo-coo-coooo! Coo-coo-roo-coo-coooo!

Wilbur: You can stop giggling now, Pippa. Tell me again what Phoebe said when you asked about the moon trip.

Pippa: 'Bout flyin' off to the edge of the universe an' endin' up where you started?

Wilbur: Yes. And the bit about her aspirations?

Pippa: "My 'ighest aspirations simply take me 'ome." What are aspirations?

Wilbur: Hopes, Pippa. Hopes and dreams. I hope people will remember Phoebe –

Pippa: Yeah, an' all the pigeons who were 'disappeared' by the TSB. Look, it's a full moon tonight, Wilbur. Why don't we fly off towards it an' see 'ow close we can get? I wonder if we might catch a glimpse of a moon pigeon!

Wilbur: Us two? Together?

Pippa: Yeah, let's see 'ow close we can get.

Wilbur: Okay. Well, we've pretty much finished Phoebe's story and our audience has gone…

Pippa: Yeah, there's jus' some 'ooman guy, pushin' a bike with a great big basket on it. No one else around. Were you countin' the chimes jus' then? I swear it was ferteen! Let's get goin', Wilbur!

. . .

Charlie: Here we go, Phoebe. Well, my little feathered friends, you're all back in Trafalgar Square. How does it feel?

Phoebe: Feels good. It's been a long time. I hope some of my old friends are still around. I'm dying to try out my wings.

Charlie: I imagine so. You've all been through such a lot. Hopefully now, after all the veterinary work, you'll soon be flying around like rockets.

Phoebe: If it's all the same to you, I think I'll give rockets a miss for a while longer yet!

Charlie: Oh, sorry, yes, I didn't mean to…

Phoebe: It's okay, Charlie. That's funny. Anyway, you'd better get this basket open so we can all have a flutter around.

Charlie: Of course. Here you go.

Phoebe: Thank you, Charlie. Oh, look at the moon! There's a couple of pigeons flying slowly across in front of it… and I swear that's Wilbur and Pippa! Goodbye, everyone. Goodbye, Charlie, and thanks so much for everything. Love you. Take care. I'm off to catch up with those moon pigeons. They might need some help finding their way home.

Other books by David Winship

The Battle of Trafalgar Square, 2018, ISBN 978-1724086884

Could Have Been Verse, 2018, ISBN 978-1981012350

ANTimatter, 2018, ISBN 978-1986340724

ANTidote, 2016, ISBN 978-1530860722

Through the Wormhole, Literally, 2015, ISBN 978-1508718406

Stirring the Grass, 2016, ISBN 978-1492952725

Off the Frame, 2001, ISBN 978-1482793833

Talking Trousers and Other Stories, 2013, ISBN 978-1484898420